Rise and Shine!

By Constance Allen • Illustrated by David Prebenna

Rise and shine! The sun is coming up!
On Sesame Street, little monsters and birds
and grouches are still snug in their beds.

Barkley is ready for an early morning walk.

The baker is baking cookies and cakes and bread.
Up and at 'em, everyone—or there won't be any left!

Ernie wakes up his buddy Bert.
"Rise and shine, Bert! The sun is coming up!"

Time to get up, Mommy and Daddy! Baby Natasha is ready to play!

In the country, Farmer Grover gets ready to milk the cows.
"Rise and shine, little cows!" he calls.

In the city, Oscar wakes up to watch the trash collectors.
"Bang those cans!" he yells. "That's it, boys! Crash 'em!
Clank 'em! Heh-heh-heh."

The Count is up early, delivering newspapers.
"One newspaper! Two newspapers! Three newspapers!"
he counts. "Rise and shine, everyone! It's a marvelous day
for counting!"

"Rise and shine!" calls Sherry Netherland.
It's time for Benny the bellhop to get to work.

Herry Monster huffs and puffs on his morning jog.

"What should I wear today?" Bert wonders.

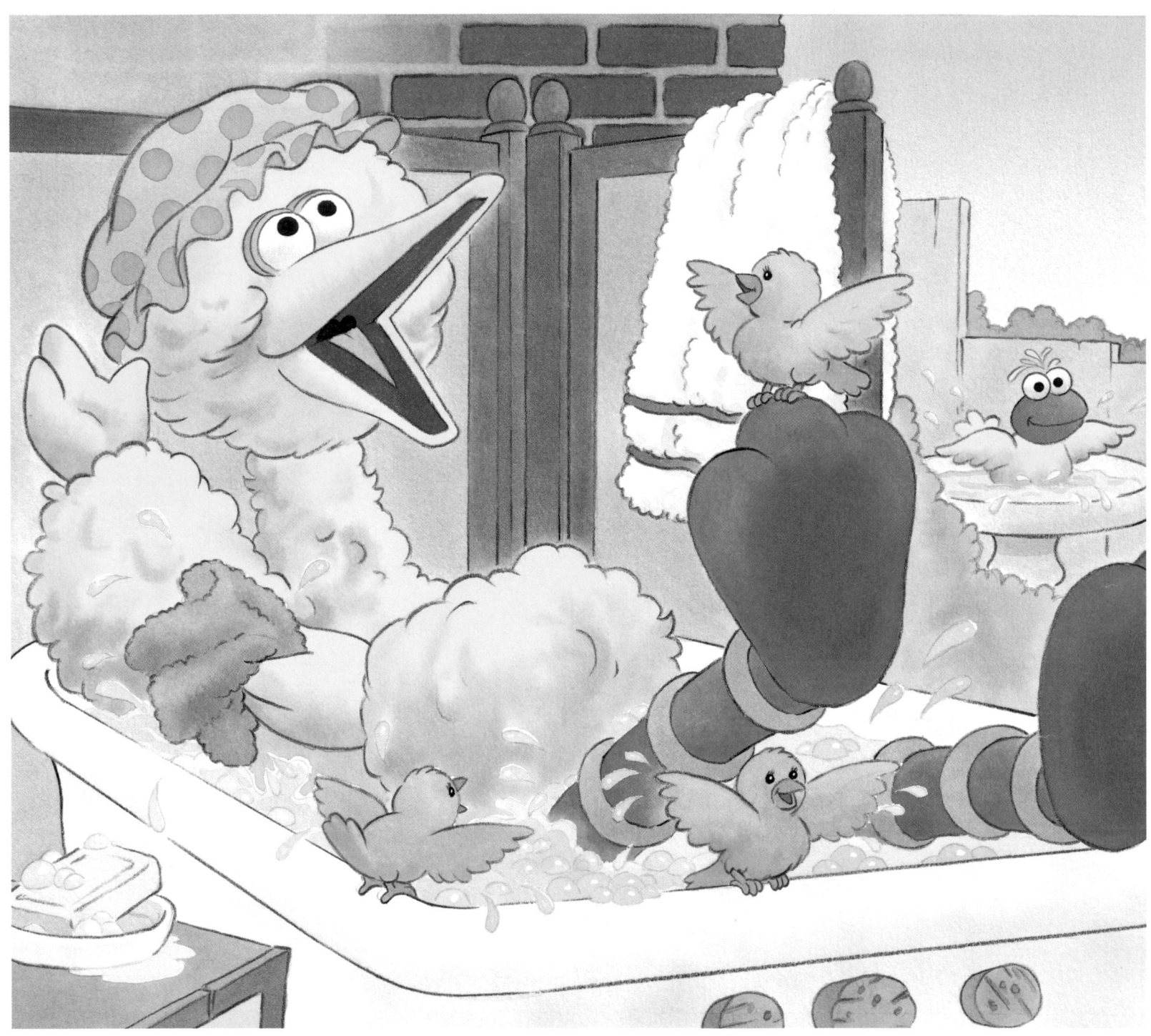

Big Bird splashes in his morning bath with some friends.
"La! La! La! La! La!" he sings as he scrubs.

Rise and shine! Breakfast is served at Hooper's Store!

Don't forget to brush your fangs!

Be sure to comb your head—and face and elbows and knees!

It's a beautiful sunny day on Sesame Street! All the monsters and birds and grouches have come out to play.

Rise and shine, little Elmo!

The End

By Constance Allen • Illustrated by David Prebenna

Me want to cook a dinner.
Me need some help from you.
Let's send the invitations.
Then lots more stuff to do!

COOKIES
TURKEY
CRANBERRIES
EGGS
FLOUR
PUMPKIN
COOKIES
POTATOES
MILK
COOKIES

First we look at recipes,
Then we make a list.
Check it over carefully.
Anything we missed?

Next we shop for groceries.
Lots of things to buy.
Can't forget the pumpkin,
So we can bake a pie.

Got to find the eggs,
Some flour and some cheese,
Turkey and cranberries...

The house look kind of messy,
Let's make it nice and neat.
Then everything look better
When we sit down to eat.

Time to do the cooking.
Let's make the stuffing first.
Me like to chop up veggies,
But onions are the worst!

Next we baste the turkey.
Then we cook the peas.
Me like to put in pepper,
But it sometimes makes me sneeze!

Time to set the table.
Would you like to do it?
Should look just like this picture.
See? There's nothing to it!

Finally our friends are here!
Let's greet them with a smile.

But not polite to eat right now.
Supposed to chat a while.

At last it time for dinner.
All guests please take a seat.
Mmmmm! It tastes delicious,
Good enough to eat!

Time to wash the dishes.
Me give the soap a squirt.
After pots and pans all done,
We get to have dessert!

Now dessert's all eaten.
There's no more — take a look!
Tummy still feels hungry…

...me gonna EAT THIS BOOK!

The End

My Baby Brother Is a Little Monster

By Sarah Albee • Illustrated by Tom Brannon

"Hi, Henry," said Big Bird. "Ready to go to the park?"

"I'm ready," replied Henry. "But my mom can't take us until my brother wakes up from his nap."

"Oh, okay," said Big Bird.

Henry sighed. "We have to play inside until he's ready."

"Nice to see you, Big Bird," said Henry's mother. "Calvin should be awake soon."

Just then, Big Bird heard a horrible noise. "Wow! What's that?" he said.

Henry rolled his eyes. "That's my brother. He's awake."

"Big Bird," said Henry, "meet Calvin."
Big Bird smiled at Calvin.
Calvin drooled and blew bubbles.

"Can we go to the park now?" Henry asked.
"In a few minutes," said Henry's mother.

"Mom, come see the cool castle we made," Henry called.
Just at that moment, Calvin dumped a box of cereal all over the floor.

While his mother was cleaning up the cereal, Calvin
crawled over and knocked down the castle.
"Gee," said Big Bird. "You want to play jacks or something?"

Henry shook his head sadly. "Nah, we can't. Calvin might try to put them in his mouth. You're not supposed to play with little toys when there's a baby around."

"Mom, now can we go to the park?" asked Henry.

"Pretty soon, honey," replied his mother. "Oh, isn't your brother adorable? Let me take a picture of the two of you together."

"Ouch!" said Henry.

"Why don't you tell him not to do that?" asked Big Bird.

"He doesn't understand that it hurts," replied Henry. "He's just a *little* monster."

"*Eeeew!* Mom!" called Henry, holding his nose. "Calvin needs to be changed!"

Henry's mother carried Calvin away to change his diaper.

"Mom, can we go to the park *now*?" Henry shouted over the noise Calvin was making.

"Soon, honey," his mother shouted back. "Calvin's hungry. I have to feed him. Then we can go."

"Your baby brother sure is loud!" yelled Big Bird.

"I wish you'd hurry up and eat that!" Henry told his brother. SPLAT! Calvin decided he was finished with his lunch. "Wow," said Big Bird. "Your baby brother sure is messy."

Henry had had enough. "I'm sick of having a baby around! He makes dumb baby noises and he messes up my toys and he throws food around.

"I wish," said Henry, his lip starting to tremble, "I wish I didn't have a baby brother!"

Henry started to cry.

"Gee," said Big Bird. "I was just thinking about how neat it would be to have a baby brother. And you taught me so much about babies today."

Henry's mother gave Henry a big hug. "I know it can be hard to have a little brother. It's okay to feel angry sometimes. Calvin is lucky to have such a patient big brother."

Henry stopped sniffling. "Really?"

"Yes, really," said his mother. "Come on! Let's go to the park!"

A little while later, as they were playing catch, Big Bird stopped. "Hey, Henry," he said softly, "I think Calvin just said your name."

Henry hurried over to Calvin. "Mom!" he shrieked. "Hey, Mom! Calvin said my name!"

Henry's mother ran over to listen, too.

"En-wee, En-wee," Calvin said.

The End

HAPPY AND SAD, GROUCHY AND GLAD

By Constance Allen • Illustrated by Tom Brannon

Oh welcome, oh welcome to our little play.
We are ever so glad you could join us today!
We are going to talk about FEELINGS! And so,
please open the curtain and on with the show!

We are two furry monsters,
one red and one blue.
We can count up to twenty
and tie our own shoes.
We can sing oh-so-sweetly—
OR SHOUT VERY LOUD!
Have you guessed how we feel?
We're both feeling PROUD!

Here's a big plate of cookies
all gooey and sweet—
with big chocolate chips!
What time do we eat?

When me have some cookies,
that make me feel GLAD!

But when the plate's empty...
    (Hmm. Maybe just one or two
    to see how they taste.
    Mmmm! Delicious!
    Gobble, gobble!)
me feel very SAD!

To show you *my* feeling
I'll do a short dance.

I feel EMBARRASSED
in polka-dot pants!

When Oscar's up late
and makes too much noise,
when people at play group
will not share their toys,
when my birdseed pancakes
turn out to be lumpy,
I sit in a corner
and feel really GRUMPY!

Pizza and ice cream,
my little pet fish,
my warm fuzzy blankie,
my favorite dish,
cute furry kitties,
and honey on toast—
these things are all nice,
but I LOVE MOMMY most!

Mumford's my name,
Many tricks I perform.
I pull rabbits from hats.
I can make a rainstorm!

A-LA-PEANUT-BUTTER SANDWICHES!

Good heavens, my rabbits
are extra-large-sized!
It's snowing, not raining—
even I feel SURPRISED!

I'm Shelley the Turtle.
I'll make my rhyme brief,
for I'm shaking and trembling
up here like a leaf!
I feel awfully SHY,
in case you can't tell,
so if nobody minds
I'll go back in my shell.

When your crayons get broken,
you've lost your new shoe,
your picnic gets rained on
you've nothing to do,
you stub your big toe,
and you have to yell OUCH!
Well, what could be better?
You feel like a GROUCH!

I *do* not like thunder and lightning, do you?
Or little white ghosts that creep up and shout, "Boo!"
Or tigers that growl and look underfed!
These make me so SCARED, I crawl under my bed!

When we're feeling HAPPY,
we stand on our heads
and we dance all around
and we jump on our beds!
We sing tra-la-la
and we laugh ho-ho-ho!
When we're feeling HAPPY,
we let the world know!

And that is the ending of our little play.
We thank you for sharing our feelings today!

The End

Just the Way You Are

By Kara McMahon • Illustrated by Joe Mathieu

"See you next week, Miss Linda!" Zoe called as she left dance class. She twirled and leaped down the street. Class might have ended, but Zoe still felt like dancing!

"I love being a ballerina," she said happily.

Whoosh! Flash! Swoosh!
"Super-Duper Elmo to the rescue!" Elmo cried.

"I don't need to be rescued!" Zoe said with a giggle. "But I do need to practice my ballet steps. Do you want to practice with me?"

"Well, Elmo *was* playing superhero...," said Elmo, "but okay. Elmo can try to practice ballet."

"Ballet dancers don't usually wear capes," Zoe explained. "So you should take off that cape."

"Watch this," Zoe instructed. She turned gracefully. "Now you try."
Elmo tried to copy Zoe, but he almost lost his balance.

"Nice try," Zoe said. "Try this instead." She leaped gracefully and landed softly.

Elmo took a running start and leaped through the air yelling, "Super-Duper Elmo!" He landed with a big thud.

"No, Elmo, that's not right!" Zoe said.

"Sorry, Zoe, but Elmo doesn't like ballet as much as you do," Elmo said. "Let's play superheroes instead, okay?"

Zoe could not believe her ears. Elmo said he didn't really like ballet! But Zoe was a ballerina. And if Elmo did not like ballet, that must mean that Elmo did not like ballerinas. Did that mean that Elmo did not like *Zoe*?

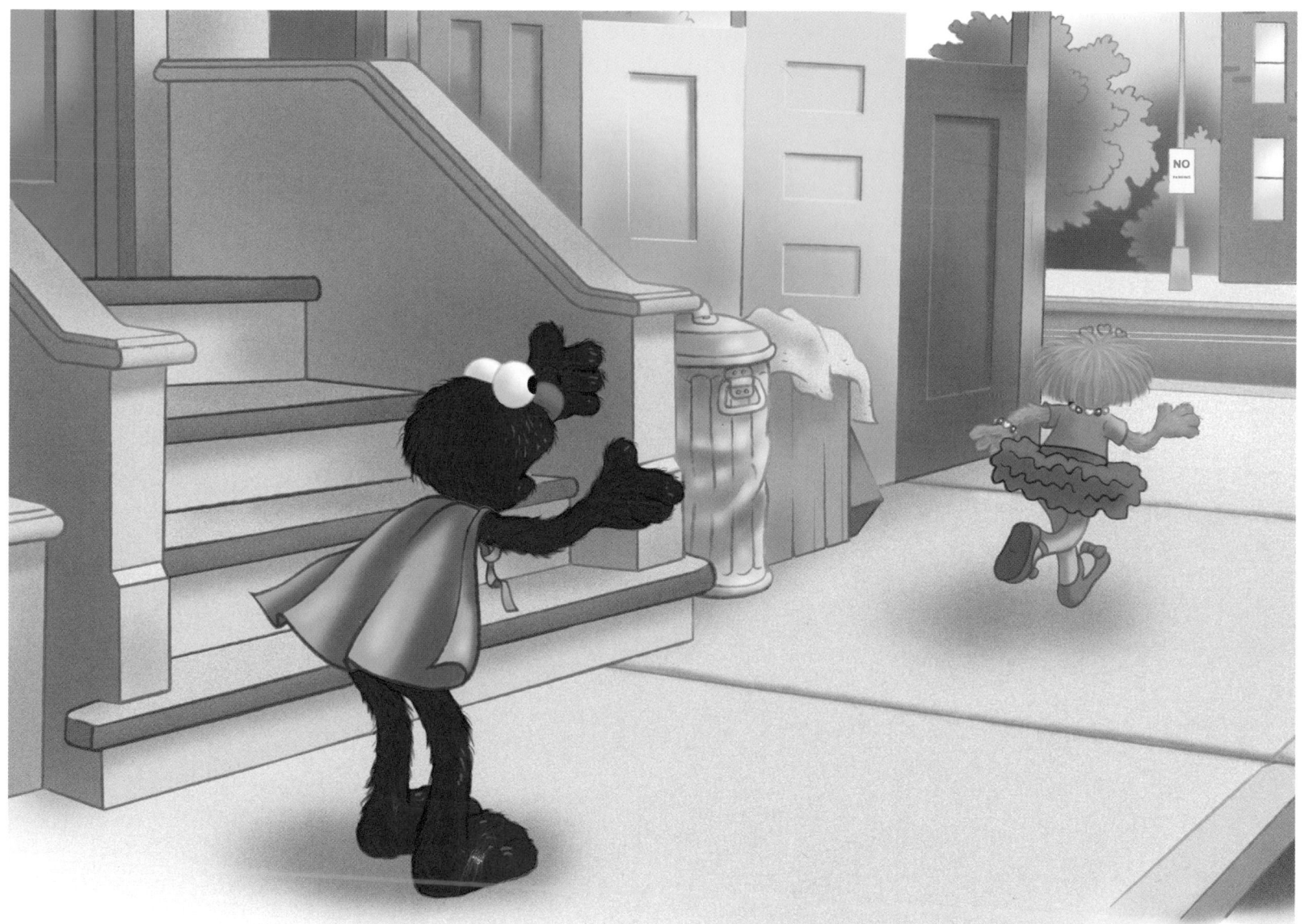

Elmo put his cape back on. "Do you have a cape you can wear?" he asked.

"Sorry, Elmo, I have to go home now," Zoe said, rushing off.

"Wait, Zoe!" Elmo called after her. "You can pretend your tutu is a cape!"

But Zoe was gone.

Zoe walked slowly down the street. She did not feel proud and happy. Instead she felt sad.

Zoe tugged on her tutu. "I really want Elmo to like me," she said to herself. "So if Elmo doesn't like ballet, then that means I can't be a ballerina anymore."

Zoe walked over to the nearest trash can. Should she throw away her beloved tutu?

"Hey, don't bother me during lunch!" a grouchy voice grumbled.

"Oh, sorry, Oscar," Zoe replied. "I didn't realize this was your can. I was just thinking about throwing away my tutu."

"This *tutu* is *too, too* nice to be trash!" Oscar said, scowling. "Why would you want to throw it away?"

"My tutu *is* trash," Zoe said sadly. "I don't want it anymore. Maybe you can use it for something."

Oscar scratched his head. *Well, if Zoe doesn't want it anymore, then I guess it is trash,* he thought.

But what could a grouch do with a tutu?
Oscar tried dangling it outside his can
as a trashy flag, but it looked too pretty.

He tried wearing it as a hat,
but it just wasn't grouchy enough.

Oscar wasn't sure
what to do with the tutu!

"Super-Duper Elmo is looking for Zoe," Elmo called as he walked by Oscar's can. "Hey, why does Oscar have Zoe's tutu?"

"It's not a tutu anymore," Oscar answered from inside his can. "It's trash!"

"This tutu is way too nice to be trash!" Elmo declared. "May Elmo have it, please?"

"Too nice? I knew it! Yuck!" Oscar popped up out of his can. "Take it! Zoe went that way. Now SCRAM!"

Elmo ran to find Zoe. "Super-Duper Elmo rescued Zoe's tutu from Oscar," he called as he ran up to his friend.

"Elmo, I *gave* the tutu to Oscar," Zoe said. "I don't want it anymore."

"But you *love* ballet!" Elmo said, sounding puzzled.
"Yes, but you don't," Zoe explained. "And since I want
you to like me, I decided I can't be a ballerina anymore."

"But Elmo *does* like Zoe!" Elmo said. "Elmo likes you just the way you are!"

"Just the way I am?" Zoe asked, still unsure. "Even as a ballerina? Even though you don't like ballet as much as I do?"

"Elmo is very sorry for hurting Zoe's feelings," said Elmo, handing Zoe her tutu. "Elmo likes Ballerina Zoe. And Elmo would like Astronaut Zoe or Farmer Zoe, too."

"Okay, Elmo!" said Zoe. "Thank you for my tutu. And I'm sorry I asked you to take off your cape."

"Hey, Elmo, I have a great idea," Zoe said as she stepped into her tutu. "We can play superheroes *and* practice ballet. And I can be Super-Duper Ballerina Zoe!"

And so she was!

The End

Sleep Tight!

By Constance Allen • Illustrated by David Prebenna

"Time to go home, Elmo!" calls Elmo's daddy.
"Just one more game of monster tag, please,
Daddy?" says Elmo.
"Okay. One more game," says Elmo's daddy.

On the way home from the park, Elmo and his daddy see lots of other people on their way home, too.

It's almost bedtime for little monsters.

On Sesame Street, everyone is getting ready for bed.
Splish, splash! Little Bird shakes his feathers in his warm bath.

Sleepy monsters comb their fur and brush their teeth.

Flossie isn't sleepy yet. Herry and Flossie do stretches.

"… Seven, eight, nine, ten," counts Herry Monster. "Are you getting sleepy, Flossie?"

Flossie shakes her head.

"Ten slow toe touches," says Herry. "One… two… three… four…"

Oscar finishes his book, *Mother Grouch Rhymes*.
"Little Boy Grouch, come blow your kazoo.
Take a mud bath and eat anchovy stew…"
He closes his book. Sleep tight, sleepy grouch.

Big Bird sings his teddy bear a lullaby.
"Rock-a-bye, Radar, snug in my nest.
Time for us both to lie down and rest!
Sleep tight, little bear," says Big Bird.

At the Snuffleupagus cave, it's bedtime for Alice.
Boing! Boing! Boing!
She bounces on the bed. Sleep tight, Alice.

In the Count's castle, the Count counts sheep.
"One sheep! Two sheep! Three beautiful woolly sheep!" cries the Count.
Sleep tight, Count.

In the country, Cowboy Grover settles down to sleep under the stars.

"Sleep tight, little cows!" he calls.

In the city, Hoots the Owl plays a saxophone serenade above the city lights.

Bee-boop-a-diddly-diddly-doo-wha-doo!

"I'll keep things cool till morning," he croons. "Sleep tight, everyone."

In Ernie's window box, sleepy Twiddlebugs
snuggle under their leaf blankets.
Sleep tight, little Twiddlebugs.

All is quiet on Sesame Street. Monsters and birds and grouches and Twiddlebugs sleep soundly in their beds.

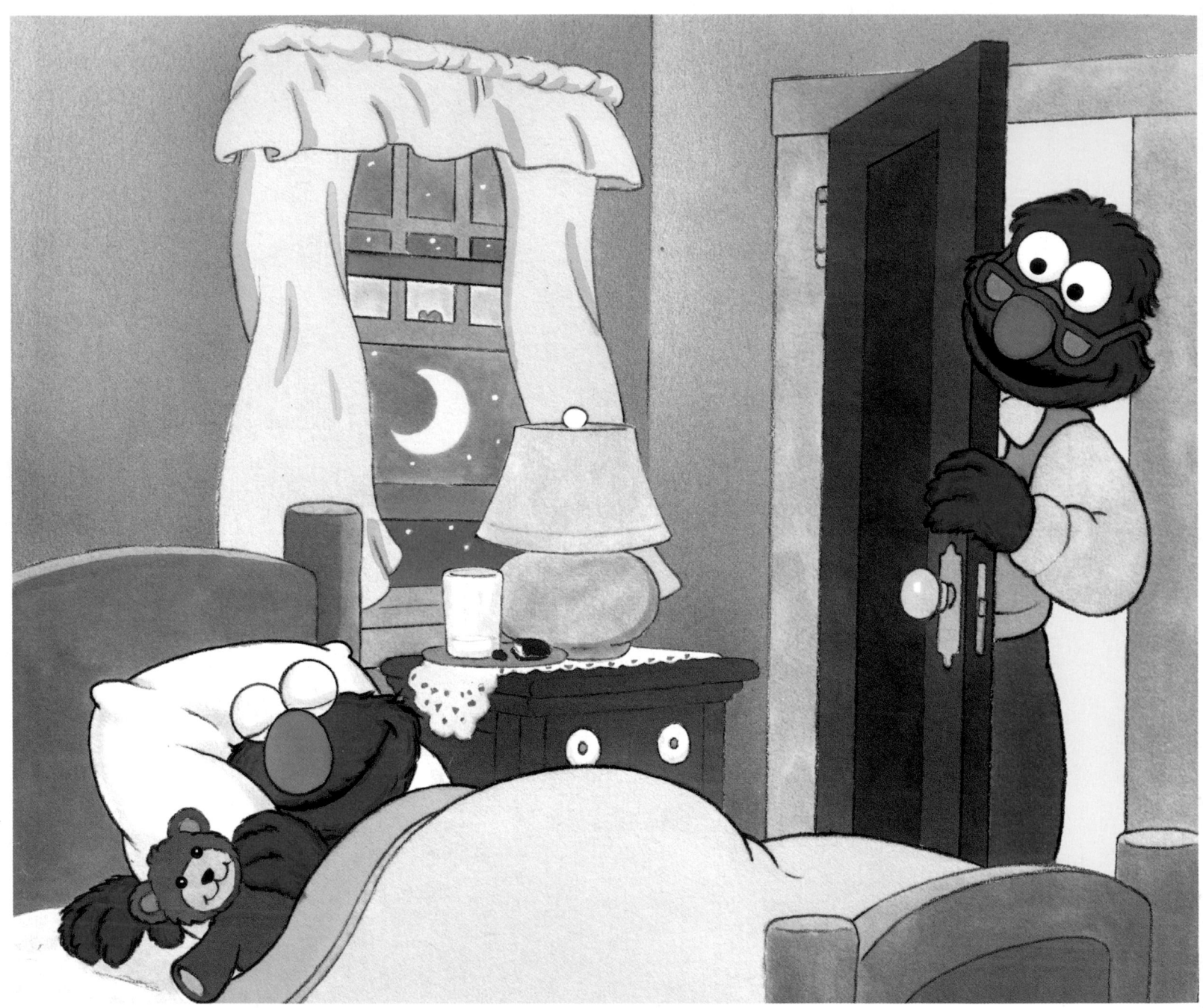

Sleep tight, little Elmo.

The End